For Gemk,

Whose endless supply of ideas and honest critique made this possible.

感謝 Gemk

源源不絕的靈感及誠懇的建議讓這一切成真。

Cool Charlie

酷查理

Coleen Reddy 著

張春英 繪

薛慧儀 譯

三民書局

Charlie is the coolest boy in school.
He has lots of cool toys and cool clothes.
He has lots of cool friends.

查理是全校最酷的男生。
他有好多酷玩具和酷衣服，
還有好多很酷的朋友。

3

But Charlie is not nice. He is mean.
He does not smile. He does not like Carl.

但是查理對待別人一點都不和氣，他總是很不友善。
他從來不微笑。而且，他討厭卡爾。

Carl is not cool. He looks geeky.
But Carl is nice and smart.
Charlie makes fun of Carl.
Charlie says, "You are so ugly.
You look like a cactus."

卡爾不但一點也不酷，而且還長得有點奇怪。
但他人很好，又很聰明。
查理常常取笑卡爾說：「你醜死了，
看起來就像棵仙人掌。」

Everybody laughs at Carl.

Carl is sad. He wants to cry.

Why is Cool Charlie so mean to Carl?

大家也都跟著嘲笑卡爾，
讓卡爾好傷心。他好想哭。
為什麼酷查理要對卡爾這麼壞呢？

9

One day, Charlie says, "Carl is so stupid."
Carl is mad. He says, "I am not stupid. I am smart."
Charlie laughs and says, "You cannot do anything.
You are not smart."

有一天，查理說：「卡爾笨死了。」
卡爾很生氣。他說：「我才不笨呢！我很聰明。」
查理哈哈大笑說：「你什麼都不會，你才不聰明呢！」

11

Carl says, "I am smart. I can do anything."

Charlie asks, "Can you do this math sum?"

Carl says, "Sure, 1000 − 1 = 999."

卡爾說：「我很聰明，我什麼都會。」
於是查理問他：「你會做這題算術嗎？」
卡爾說：「當然！一千減一等於九百九十九。」

Cool Charlie says, "Okay, but can you read this big book in one minute?" Carl says, "Sure, watch me." Carl reads the big book in one minute. "WOW!" says everyone.

酷查理說：「就算你會吧。但你ㄐ以在一分鐘之內讀完這一大本書嗎？」
卡爾說：「當然，看我的！」卡爾真的在一分鐘之內就把書讀完了。
「哇喔！」所有的人都發出了驚嘆聲。

Cool Charlie sees a flying cockroach.
He asks, "Can you catch that cockroach?"
Carl says, "Yes, I can." He jumps up and
catches the cockroach!

16

酷查理看見一隻蟑螂飛過。

他問：「你可以捉住那隻蟑螂嗎？」

卡爾說：「可以，沒問題。」

他跳起來，一下子就捉到那隻蟑螂！

But Cool Charlie is still not happy.

He asks, "Can you cook that cockroach?"

The other boys and girls say, "That's stupid.

No one can cook a cockroach."

But Carl says, "Yes, I can. I can cook anything.

I can cook a cockroach."

Carl cooks the cockroach.

但酷查理還是不高興，他問：「你敢煮了那隻蟑螂嗎？」
其他的男生女生們說：「真蠢，哪有人煮蟑螂的？」
但卡爾說：「可以啊！我能煮任何東西，當然也可以煮蟑螂。」
卡爾真的煮了那隻蟑螂。

Cool Charlie says, "That's nothing. Can you walk on the school roof?"
"Ooh!" says everyone. It is dangerous to walk on a roof.
Carl looks unhappy. He is not sure.
Cool Charlie starts laughing again.

酷查理說：「那不算什麼，你可以在學校屋頂上走嗎？」
「喔！」大家驚嘆地說。在屋頂上走很危險呢！
卡爾看起來不太高興。他不確定自己能不能做到。
酷查理又開始笑了起來。

Carl says, "Yes, I can. I can walk on the roof."
Everybody watches Carl.
Carl climbs onto the roof.

He walks on the roof.

OH NO!

He
falls
off
the
roof!

卡爾說：「沒問題，我可以在屋頂上走。」
每個人都睜大眼睛看著卡爾。
卡爾爬上屋頂，開始在屋頂上走著。
喔！糟了！他從屋頂上摔下來了！

Everybody runs to Carl.

His eyes are closed.

Cool Charlie is scared.

"I'm sorry, I'm sorry," he says.

But still Carl does not open his eyes.

大家都跑到卡爾身邊。他的眼睛是閉著的。

酷查理嚇壞了，一直說：「對不起！對不起！」

但卡爾還是沒有張開眼睛。

The teacher is there.
She asks, "What happened?"
The children tell her.
The teacher says that Carl will be okay.

老師過來了。
她問：「怎麼了？」
孩子們把剛才發生的事報告給老師聽。
老師說卡爾應該不會有事。

27

The teacher says, "It is not cool to be mean.
You must say 'sorry' to Carl."
Charlie is sad.
He says, "Sorry, please forgive me."
Carl opens his eyes and smiles.

老師對酷查理說：「耍壞一點也不酷。
你一定得向卡爾說『對不起』。」
查理很難過，他對卡爾說：「對不起，請你原諒我。」
卡爾張開眼睛，露出了微笑。

"I will if you can do something for me."

"Anything, I will do anything."

"You must eat the **cockroach** that I cooked."

「如果你為我做一件事，我就原諒你。」
「任何事情都可以！我都會去做！」
「你得把我剛才煮的那隻蟑螂吃掉。」

31

Charlie looks very sad.

"Okay," he says.

Carl laughs. "Just kidding!" he says.

32

Ha ha ha...

查理看起來很難過，他說：「好吧。」
卡爾笑了起來，他說：「只是開玩笑啦！」

小朋友，你會用英文說＋－×÷嗎？讓我們來告訴你到底該怎麼說！首先按下 track 3 來看看有哪些單字。

 plus [plʌs]　　　　　 minus [ˋmaɪnəs]

 times [taɪmz]　　　　 divide [dəˋvaɪd]

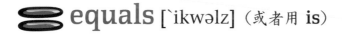 equals [ˋikwəlz]（或者用 is）

現在按下 track 4，讓我們帶你一起來念下面四題：

6 ＋ 2 = 8 (six plus two equals eight)

10 － 3 = 7 (ten minus three equals seven)

4 × 5 = 20 (four times five equals twenty)

20 ÷ 5 = 4 (twenty divided by five equals four)

你都會了嗎？下面有幾題練習題，按下 track 5，我們會把數字的部分念出來，在聽的時候，要由你自己來把空格部分的單字大聲地念出來，準備好了嗎？開始！！

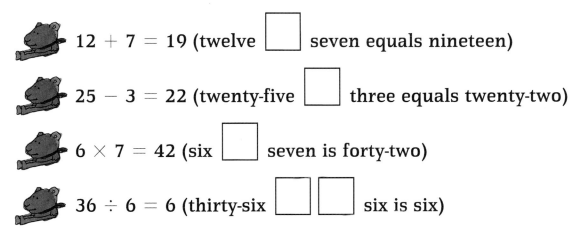

$12 + 7 = 19$ (twelve ☐ seven equals nineteen)

$25 - 3 = 22$ (twenty-five ☐ three equals twenty-two)

$6 \times 7 = 42$ (six ☐ seven is forty-two)

$36 \div 6 = 6$ (thirty-six ☐ ☐ six is six)

都答對了嗎？可以按下 track 6 來聽正確答案喔！

※答案：plus, minus, times, divided by

35

全新創作 英文讀本
帶給你優格（yogurt）般，青春的酸甜滋味！

Teens' Chronicles

愛閱雙語叢書

青春記事簿

大維的驚奇派對／秀寶貝，說故事／杰生的大秘密
傑克的戀愛初體驗／誰是他爸爸？
叛逆大維打工記／外星老師來上課／耶！放假了！

你我身上純真的影子，
透過一篇篇幽默風趣的故事重現，
推薦你這套青春無悔的創作系列，
讓愛玫、杰生、大維、凱爾、海倫、傑克，
帶你進入他們的世界，品味另一種學習英語的全新感受。

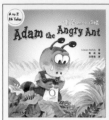

A to Z
26 Tales

二十六個妙朋友，陪你一起

愛閱雙語叢書

✿26個妙朋友系列✿

二十六個英文字母，二十六冊有趣的讀本，最適合初學英文的你！

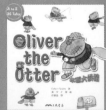

快樂學英文！

精心錄製的雙語CD，
　　讓孩子學會正確的英文發音
用心構思的故事情節，
　　讓兒童熟悉生活中常見的單字
特別設計的親子活動，
　　讓家長和小朋友一起動動手、動動腦

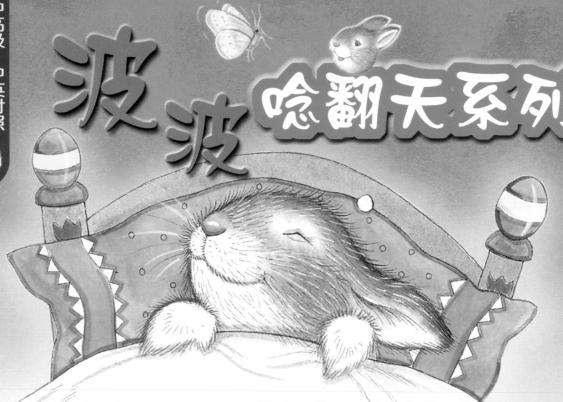

波波唸翻天系列

你知道可愛的小兔子也會 "碎碎唸" 嗎？

波波就是這樣。

他將要告訴我們什麼有趣的故事呢？

波波的復活節／波波的西部冒險記／波波上課記／我愛你，波波

波波的下雪天／波波郊遊去／波波打球記／聖誕快樂，波波／波波的萬聖夜

共 9 本，每本均附 CD

國家圖書館出版品預行編目資料

Cool Charlie:酷查理 / Coleen Reddy著; 張春英繪;
薛慧儀譯.－－初版一刷.－－臺北市; 三民,
2003
　　面; 　公分－－(愛閱雙語叢書.二十六個妙朋
友系列) 中英對照
ISBN 957－14－3776－X 　(精裝)

1.英國語言－讀本

523.38　　　　　　　　　　　　　92008842

© 　Cool Charlie
　　　　　——酷查理

著作人　Coleen Reddy
繪　圖　張春英
譯　者　薛慧儀
發行人　劉振強
著作財　三民書局股份有限公司
產權人　臺北市復興北路386號
發行所　三民書局股份有限公司
　　　　地址／臺北市復興北路386號
　　　　電話／(02)25006600
　　　　郵撥／0009998－5
印刷所　三民書局股份有限公司
門市部　復北店／臺北市復興北路386號
　　　　重南店／臺北市重慶南路一段61號
初版一刷　2003年7月
編　號　S 85636－1
定　價　新臺幣壹佰捌拾元整
行政院新聞局登記證局版臺業字第○二○○號

ISBN　957－14－3776－X 　(精裝)